This book belongs to

_____

_____

For Rupert and Erin
(And with thanks to Peter Perspective)
C.F.

This book is printed on paper produced from
wood that comes from sustainably managed forests

First published in Great Britain in 2011 by
Gullane Children's Books
185 Fleet Street, London, EC4A 2HS
www.gullanebooks.com

1   3   5   7   9   10   8   6   4   2

Text and illustrations © Charles Fuge 2011

ISBN:978-1-86233-811-1

Printed and bound in China

Charles Fuge's
Astonishing Animal
ABC

GULLANE
CHILDREN'S BOOKS

A, arty aardvark,

B, bouncing bear,

C, cosy cobra,
curled up in a
comfy chair.

D, dancing dodo,

E, enormous egg,

F, fat flamingo,
feeling frightened,
on one leg.

G,
girl gorilla,

H and **I,**
hare on ice,

J, jolly jackal,
and his jelly-jumping mice.

K, king koala,

L, lion's lost,

M, mouse at market, asking, "What do mammoths cost?"

N, nasty narwhal,

O, outraged owl,

P, pirate penguin
and his panther,
on the prowl.

Q, quite quiet quail,

R, rhino row,

S, snoozy sloth needs sleep

and wants some silence **NOW!**

T, tortoise training

U, unicorn,

V, vulture visits vet

(a Viking vole named Vaughn).

x-ray department →

W, worried walrus,

X and Y,
x-ray yak,

and **Z** is a zooming...

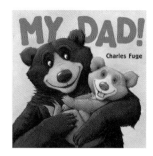

Other books by
Charles Fuge

Blot and Og's Monster Party
WRITTEN BY Tasha Pym

This is the Way

My Dad!

I Know a Rhino

Yip! Snap! Yap!

What Can a Baby Do?
WRITTEN BY Sarah Churchill

Little Wombat books

Sometimes I Like to Curl up in a Ball
WRITTEN BY Vicki Churchill

Found You, Little Wombat!
WRITTEN BY Angela McAllister

Where to, Little Wombat?

Swim, Little Wombat, Swim!

Watch Out, Little Wombat!

The Adventures of Little Wombat!
A collection of four fun-filled tales

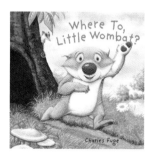